Katie Kazoo,
SWITCHEROO

Anyone But Me

for Ian B.

Library of Congress Catalog Card Number: 2002102949

10 9 8 7 6 5 4 3 2 1

Proprietary ISBN 978-1-101-95129-3
Part of Boxed Set, ISBN 978-1-101-95128-6

Katie Kazoo, SWITCHEROO

Anyone But Me

by Nancy Krulik • illustrated by John & Wendy

Grosset & Dunlap

Chapter 1

"I've got it! I've got it!"

The football soared right toward Katie Carew. She ran toward the ball, reached out her hands and . . . *oomph!* She missed it completely.

"You took your eyes off it again," Katie's best friend, Jeremy Fox, said, jogging up to her. He pushed his thin wire glasses higher up on his nose and ran his hands through his curly brown hair.

"I know," Katie replied simply. What else could she say?

"Katie, I can't believe you did that!" Kevin Camilleri shouted across the field. "You lost the whole game for us."

Just then George Brennan came charging across the field. He had a big smile on his face. Katie groaned. Of course George was happy. His team had just won the game—thanks to Katie's fumble!

"Don't yell at the secret weapon," George told Kevin.

"Secret weapon? Are you kidding?" Kevin asked. "Secret weapons help *win* games, George."

"Exactly," George agreed. "Katie's the secret weapon for *our* team!"

Katie blinked her eyes tight. She didn't want George to see her cry.

"Forget about George," Jeremy whispered to Katie. "He can't help being mean. He was just born that way."

Katie tried to smile. "Could be," she said.

The truth was, Katie wasn't really sure why George was nasty to everyone in class 3A. Most new kids tried to make friends. Not

George. He tried to make enemies.

Just then, Katie's other best friend, Suzanne Lock, ran across the playground to them. "Let's go play on the monkey bars for a while," she suggested, pulling Katie and Jeremy away from George. "I'll bet I can hang upside down longer than either of you."

Katie stared at Suzanne. Her friend was wearing a skirt! "You're going to turn upside down in *that*?" Katie asked.

"Sure!" Suzanne said, yanking her skirt up to her bellybutton.

Katie's mouth flew open.

Jeremy blushed.

"It's okay, you guys," Suzanne laughed. "See, I'm wearing shorts under here. This way I can wear a skirt and still play."

Katie laughed. Leave it to Suzanne to find a way to look pretty and still hang upside down on the jungle gym.

"Okay! Last one at the monkey bars is a rotten egg," Katie called as she dashed away.

Suzanne and Jeremy took off after Katie. Katie held on to her lead, but not for long. Jeremy was the fastest runner in the class. He quickly pulled up next to Katie. Katie took a deep breath. She moved her feet faster than ever. But not fast enough. Jeremy zoomed into the lead.

Katie frowned. Well, at least she was ahead of Suzanne. Katie turned her head to see just how far behind Suzanne was and . . .

Splat!

Katie stepped right into a big, wet puddle. Gushy brown mud splashed all over her. Katie stopped running and looked down at her jeans.

"Oh, no!" she cried out. "What a mess!"

Katie wasn't kidding. She was a total mess. There were mud splatters all over her jeans. Her *favorite* jeans—the ones with the pink and blue flowers embroidered all over them.

If this were first grade, Katie could have changed into the clean clothes in her cubby. But Katie was in third grade now. Nobody in third grade kept a change of clothes at school. That was for babies. Katie was going to have to wear her mud-stained jeans for the whole rest of the day.

"Nice one, Carew," George shouted across the yard. "Check it out, everybody! There's a Mud Monster in the playground."

George stuck his arms straight out and walked around the yard pretending to be Frankenstein. The other kids laughed.

Katie wanted to cry. This was the worst recess ever. She wished Mrs. Derkman would blow her whistle and make everyone go in to class. Even doing schoolwork had to be better than this!

"George, go away or I'm gonna tell," Suzanne warned as she ran over to defend her friend.

A big smile formed on George's chubby, round face. "Yeah, like I'm real scared," he laughed while he pretended to tremble. "What's Mrs. *Jerkman* going to do? Call my mommy?"

Katie and Suzanne stared at George in

amazement. He'd just called their teacher, Mrs. Derkman, a mean name—and he hadn't even whispered it! He didn't seem scared to have the teacher phone his mom, either.

Before Katie or Suzanne could answer George, Mrs. Derkman blew her red whistle three times.

Phew! Recess was over. It was time to go back to class. Katie was very glad. She used her hands to wipe off some of the mud, and then ran to line up.

"You okay?" Jeremy whispered to Katie.

"I guess," Katie replied.

"George is a creep. You know that."

Katie nodded. But knowing that wasn't going to make George stop calling her the Mud Monster. He'd probably go at it all day, unless . . .

Katie couldn't help wishing that some-one else would do something embarrassing that afternoon. Then maybe George Brennan would tease that kid instead.

Chapter 2

"This is for you," Kevin whispered to Katie. He handed her a note. It was written on light-blue paper and folded up really small. Katie knew it was from Suzanne. Her notes always looked like that.

"If you have an answer for her, send it yourself," Kevin told Katie. "I don't want to get into trouble again."

Katie understood. Kevin sat at the desk right between Suzanne and Katie. He always wound up passing notes from girl to girl. Yesterday, Mrs. Derkman had caught Kevin passing a note from Katie to Suzanne. Kevin had had to write an apology note to Mrs. Derkman.

Katie unfolded the paper. *Do you want to come over after school?* the note read.

Katie scribbled her answer on the bottom of the note. *No, thanks. I have to go home and change. Maybe tomorrow?*

Katie tossed the paper over Kevin's head. It landed right on Suzanne's desk. Katie crossed her fingers, hoping Mrs. Derkman didn't see.

Katie lucked out. Mrs. Derkman didn't notice the flying note. She was too busy writing on the board.

"Okay, take out your pencils and math notebooks. Today we're going to review subtraction with borrowing," the teacher announced.

Katie gulped. Whenever Mrs. Derkman said the word "review," it meant that she was going to ask some of the kids in the class to go to the board and solve the problems in front of everyone.

Katie slid down low in her chair, hoping

Mrs. Derkman wouldn't notice her. She didn't want to be one of the kids who were called on. It wasn't that Katie couldn't do subtraction with borrowing. It was more that she hated being in front of the whole class.

"I'll try one, Mrs. Derkman," Suzanne volunteered.

Katie sighed. Suzanne never worried about making a mistake in front of the whole class. She just liked being the center of attention. Katie wished she could be more like that.

But today, Mrs. Derkman didn't ask Suzanne to come up to the board. She picked Mandy Banks, Zoe Canter, and Jeremy instead. Mandy went first. She whizzed through her problem. No surprise there—she was like a computer when it came to math. Next it was Zoe's turn.

"All right, Zoe," Mrs. Derkman said as Zoe walked up to the board. "What will you get when you subtract 152 from 901?"

"The wrong answer!" George joked out loud.

Some kids in the class giggled. Zoe blushed.

Katie thought it was really mean of George to joke around like that. Everyone knew Zoe had a lot of trouble with math.

Mrs. Derkman looked sternly over at George, but she smiled at Zoe. "Go ahead," she said to her. "We'll do it together."

When it was his turn, Jeremy took his time solving the subtraction problem. Katie smiled. That was Jeremy: slow and steady like the tortoise in the story of *The Tortoise and the Hare*.

Sometimes Jeremy's careful slowness could get kind of annoying. But not today. *As long as Jeremy's up there, Mrs. Derkman won't call on me,* Katie thought to herself.

$$33+16=$$
$$88-32=$$
$$67-11=$$

But eventually Jeremy did finish the problem. And he got the right answer . . . as usual.

Mrs. Derkman smiled and wrote another math problem on the board. "Let's do one more," she said.

Katie sunk even lower in her chair. Her lip was practically resting on her desk. But it was no use. Mrs. Derkman saw her anyway.

"Katie, will you solve this for us?" the teacher asked.

Katie sighed. She stood up and slowly walked toward the board.

"Here comes the Mud Monster!" Katie heard George whisper as she walked past his desk. Katie didn't want to walk past George, but she had no choice. He sat right in the front row—where Mrs. Derkman could keep an eye on him.

Katie reached the board and picked up a piece of yellow chalk. She opened her mouth to take a deep, calming breath. But instead of breathing in air, she let out a great big belch.

It was the loudest burp she'd ever heard.
A real record-breaker.

The other kids in class began to laugh.
Katie blushed beet red. "I'm sorry," she
apologized to Mrs. Derkman. Katie didn't
want her teacher to think she'd done that
on purpose.

Out of the corner of her eye, Katie could
see George holding his nose. He was pretending
to die from the smell of her breath.

"Katie's stinking up the classroom!"
George exclaimed. He laughed so hard, he
nearly fell off his chair.

Chapter 3

For the rest of that day, everywhere Katie looked, someone was laughing at her. Mostly because George kept cracking jokes.

"Hey, Mud Monster, can you burp a song for us?" he asked. "I can." George began to belch out the ABC song. By the time he got to Z, the other kids were all giggling.

"Hey, you know something?" George announced. "Burping a song kinda sounds like a kazoo. That's what your name should be, Katie. Not Katie Carew. Katie *Kazoo*!" Then he started chanting, "Katie Kazoo, Katie Kazoo," over and over again.

The other kids began to join in. "Katie

Kazoo. Katie Kazoo. Katie Kazoo. Katie Kazoo!"

Katie sank down in her chair. She tried hard not to cry.

"All right, that's enough," Mrs. Derkman scolded the class. She turned to George. "I'm sending a note home to your mother. I expect you to bring it back to me with her signature."

George shrugged as if he didn't care.

As the afternoon went on, Katie wished the other kids would stop laughing when George teased her. He really wasn't all that funny. But she did kind of understand why the kids kept laughing. If they didn't, George might make fun of them next.

Before school ended, Katie walked over toward the window, where the hamster cage was. It was her turn to feed Speedy this week.

Hamsters are so lucky, Katie thought to herself as she watched Speedy running on his wheel. *They never have bad days. Every day is just the same for them.*

Finally, the bell rang. The day was over. Katie grabbed her books and ran for the door. She had to make sure she was the first one out of the classroom.

But it didn't matter. George caught up to Katie right away. He followed her halfway home. "Katie Kazoo, I see you!" he shouted.

"Hey, Katie, wait up!"

Katie could hear Jeremy calling after her as she ran towards her house. She knew he just wanted to make her feel better. But Katie didn't stop. She didn't want to hang out with Jeremy. She just wanted to get home, go upstairs to her room, and shut the door.

Even that wasn't easy to do. When Katie got home, her mother was sitting on the front steps, waiting for her.

"Hi, Kat!" Her mother greeted her with her special nickname. "I made some yummy chocolate-chip cookies. Want some?"

"I, um, I'm not hungry right now," Katie mumbled. She raced past her and opened the screen door. "I gotta get homework done."

As Katie entered her room, she found her brown-and-white cocker spaniel, Pepper, lying on her bed. Pepper picked up his head and looked at Katie. He reached out his long, pink tongue and gave her a big kiss. Katie hugged her dog tightly.

"Thanks, Pepper," she whispered quietly into his brown floppy ear. "At least *someone* isn't making fun of me today."

Pepper looked up at her and smiled.

Jeremy was always telling Katie that dogs couldn't really smile. But Katie was sure that Pepper could. "Pepper's just a really special dog," she would tell Jeremy when he argued with her. "He's even smarter than people."

Now, as Pepper lay his head in her lap,

Katie decided that even if her cocker spaniel wasn't smarter than people, he certainly was nicer.

That night at dinner, Katie picked at her spaghetti. She rolled the long noodles around on her fork. Then she pushed the meatballs over to the side of her plate and scowled.

Three weeks ago, Katie had told her mother that she was a vegetarian. Her mother kept giving her meat anyway. Well, Katie was just not going to eat the meatballs, that's all.

"You wouldn't believe the day I had at the office," Katie's father announced as he took a bite of his meatball. "We have this new guy, and he was working on the computer when . . ."

Usually Katie hated it when her father took up the whole dinner talking about his accounting firm. But tonight she was happy to sit quietly and let him talk. It was better than having to explain why she was so miserable.

Unfortunately, her dad's story finally

came to an end. Immediately, Katie's mother changed the subject. "So, Kat, what's new with you?" she asked.

Katie shrugged. "Nothing."

"Really?" her mother asked. "Well, you sure had a lot of homework. I haven't seen you since you got home."

Katie nodded slowly. "We had a ton of social studies questions," she muttered. "Um . . . I'm not so hungry. Can I be excused?"

Katie watched as her parents gave each other their "nervous" looks. They knew something was wrong. They just weren't sure what to do about it. Finally, her mother said, "Sure, Kat. Go ahead. I'll clear the table."

Katie stood up and walked out of the room. She opened the front door, and sat on the stoop outside her house. She looked out into the darkness. Suddenly the whole rotten day flashed in front of her eyes.

She thought about missing the football and losing the game for her team.

She thought about her new jeans in the hamper, all caked with mud.

She thought about the belch she'd let out during math.

Worst of all, she thought about what George was going to do to her tomorrow.

"I wish I could be anyone but me!" she shouted out loud.

A shooting star shot across the dark night sky. But Katie was too upset to notice it.

Chapter 4

"Rise and shine, Katie! You're going to be late for school!" Katie's mother called from the kitchen.

Katie sat up slowly and rubbed the sleep from her eyes. She squinted at the Mickey Mouse clock on her wall. Mickey's hands were on the 8 and the 3. Oh no! It was already 8:15. School started at 8:45. She only had half an hour to get dressed, eat breakfast, and walk to school. This day was starting out really lousy.

Her mother had put out Katie's clothes for the day—a bright yellow satiny blouse and black jeans. The outfit was very cheerful.

But Katie wasn't feeling cheerful today. She went to her closet and pulled out a gray sweatshirt and jeans instead. That's how she felt. *Blech.* Like a gray, cloudy day.

As Katie came into the kitchen, her mother noticed her new outfit. "Not in the mood for yellow, huh kiddo?" she asked kindly.

Katie shook her head.

"Did you have an argument with Suzanne or Jeremy?" her mother guessed.

"No," Katie answered.

"So what's wrong?" her mother asked.

Katie thought about telling her mother what had happened yesterday. But she was afraid that her mom would call the school to complain about George's bullying. Imagine how mean George would be to her if *that* happened!

"Nothing's wrong," Katie lied to her mother. "I'm just tired."

Her mom didn't say anything. But Katie could tell she didn't believe her.

"You'd better eat that toast," her mom said. "It's getting late."

Katie nodded and slowly took a nibble of her bread. She slowly chewed each tiny bite until the toast practically melted in her mouth.

Katie *wanted* to be late.

If she arrived after the bell rang, the class would all be seated and doing their work by the time she got there. Mrs. Derkman would be upset that she was late. But it was worth it if she could avoid even a little bit of George's teasing. Definitely.

"You've got to get going," Katie's mother warned her. "You can eat the rest on the way."

Katie didn't say anything. She slipped on her backpack and headed for the door.

"Have a good day, kiddo," her mother called.

By the time Katie finally reached the school, everyone was inside the building. Katie stood outside by her classroom window. She watched as her classmates scrambled into

24

their seats. Katie knew she should hurry inside. But her feet just didn't seem to want to move.

Just then, the wind began to blow. It started out as a slow and gentle breeze. But within seconds the wind was swirling round and

round like a tornado. The weird thing was that the wild wind was only blowing around Katie. The leaves on the trees weren't moving. The bushes weren't moving. Even the flag up on the flagpole wasn't moving.

What was going on? Katie was really scared. She wished she were inside. Away from this wind. She hugged herself tightly, and closed her eyes.

And then, suddenly, everything was calm again. The wind had disappeared as quickly as it had started. Katie stood perfectly still for a moment, waiting to see if it would start up again. Finally, when she was sure the storm was over, Katie slowly opened her eyes.

Everything seemed blurry. Katie blinked really hard. Nothing changed. She still couldn't see very well.

But she could smell *really* well. And her nose was twitching. Katie stood up tall and sniffed at the air. All around her were yucky smells: salami, egg salad, old sneakers. It was hard to tell where each smell was coming from. The scents were all mixing together.

Katie hadn't only become a champion smeller. She could also hear really well. *Too* well, in fact. Everyone in the classroom seemed to be shouting. All the noise was making her nervous. Katie could feel her heart beating really, really fast.

Now Katie was really scared. She wanted to

run right home. But her parents were probably at work by now. There was no one at home to take care of her. If Katie didn't show up at school, Mrs. Derkman would phone her mother for sure. Katie definitely did not want that to happen. She ran towards the classroom. She'd have to hope her sight got better.

Bam! She bashed right into a solid glass wall.

That was weird, Katie thought. *There hadn't been a glass wall there before.*

"What's going on here?" Katie cried out.

Nobody answered. All the kids in the classroom were so busy yelling, they couldn't hear Katie's cries.

"Hello!" Katie shouted. "Can anyone hear me?"

Katie began running wildly in circles. She didn't get very far before she bashed head first into another glass wall. *Ouch!* That one really hurt.

As she reached up to rub her head, Katie

noticed that her hand looked strange. This
hand was small and furry. This hand had nails

 that really needed to be
clipped. Katie touched her
face. Her cheeks felt big
and round like huge empty pouches, and her
face was all hairy!

Quickly, Katie looked down at her body.
"Aaah!" she cried out. "I'm naked!"

Actually, she wasn't completely naked. Her
back and stomach were covered with orange-
brown fur!

And that's when Katie realized what had
happened. She wasn't outside anymore. She
was inside—in a hamster cage. She'd become
Speedy, the class hamster.

Katie tried to
scream, but the
only sound that
came out of her
mouth was a loud
squeak.

Chapter 5

"Hey, look at Speedy!" Zoe Canter called out from the other side of the glass. "He's going crazy!"

Within seconds, eighteen pairs of giant eyes were peering through the glass window. They were all staring at Katie.

Katie was really confused. How could this have happened? It didn't make any sense. People didn't just turn into hamsters.

Then Katie remembered. She'd made that wish the night before. She'd said she wanted to be anyone but herself!

"Why did *this* have to be my first wish to come true?" Katie yelped. (Of course, to the kids in class 3A, her words sounded more like "Squeak, squeak squeak, squeak squeak!")

"Somebody should throw some oil on that hamster!" George exclaimed. "That'll stop his squeaking."

"Oh, George, be quiet," Suzanne told him. "Something is obviously bothering the little guy. We should try and help him."

"It figures a rat would want to help a hamster," George said. "You're both in the same family."

"Cut it out," Suzanne replied.

"Hey, Ratgirl, show us your tail," George teased.

Katie wished she could help Suzanne, but she was just a little hamster. Luckily, George had to stop when Mrs. Derkman told them all to sit back down.

"I've got to get out of this cage," Katie squeaked to herself.

The problem was that she knew there wasn't any way out. The only opening in the cage

was at the top, and that was covered by a
screened lid. The lid was Mrs. Derkman's way
of making sure Speedy didn't escape. Now the
lid was making sure Katie didn't escape, either.

There had to be some way to get that lid off. Katie might have a hamster body now, but she still had a human brain. She was smart enough to get out of a hamster cage. She just had to come up with a plan.

Before she could think about anything, though, she had to deal with her teeth. They were feeling really long. She needed to chew on something—and fast! Quickly, Katie scampered over to a small pile of brightly colored pieces of wood.

"Ahh, that feels better." Katie sighed as she bit into a bright green chew stick. She could feel her teeth getting shorter with each nibble.

Suddenly Katie had an idea. She took the green chew stick in her mouth and placed it on top of a yellow one. Then she grabbed a blue stick and placed it on top of the green one.

If I can just build this high enough, maybe I can climb up and push the lid off, Katie thought to herself, as she took an orange chew stick and added it to the pile.

It took a while, but at last Katie built what had to be the biggest chew-stick ladder of all time. (It also was probably the *only* chew-stick ladder of all time!) If Katie could climb to the top of the pile, she might be able to reach the lid.

"Hey, look what Speedy made," she heard Manny Gonzalez whisper to Kevin.

"Cool!" Kevin agreed. "It's like a chew-stick mountain."

Katie licked her little front paws and admired her work. She took a deep breath. It was time to try out her plan. Carefully, Katie stepped onto the bottom chew stick. *So far so good,* she thought.

Once Katie was safely on the first rung of the ladder, she stood tall on her hind legs and tried to pull herself up to the next rung.

Bonk! The entire pile of chew sticks came crashing down on top of Katie's head. Luckily, the sticks were made of a soft wood. Katie wasn't hurt. And it was kind of fun eating her way out of the pile of chew sticks.

"I have to stop this!" Katie said to herself as she chewed. "I'll never get out of here if I don't stop thinking like a hamster."

The trouble was, Katie *was* a hamster. And right then she suddenly couldn't think about anything but Speedy's hamster wheel. Katie couldn't explain why she suddenly needed to run so badly. She just did. She couldn't help herself.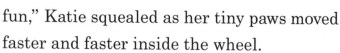

"Hey, this is fun," Katie squealed as her tiny paws moved faster and faster inside the wheel.

The wheel squeaked very loudly as Katie ran. The noise didn't bother Katie's sensitive hamster ears. In fact, she kind of liked it. Mrs. Derkman, on the other hand, didn't like the squeaking at all.

"Suzanne, will you please put a carrot in Speedy's cage?" Mrs. Derkman asked. "Maybe that will get him to stop running on that squeaky wheel."

"Yes, Mrs. Derkman," Suzanne said.

Katie watched as her best friend walked over, lifted the lid off the cage, and dropped in a carrot.

Katie leaped from the wheel and grabbed the treat. As she chewed the carrot, Katie looked up gratefully at Suzanne. Her friend had given Katie more than just a snack. She'd given her a great idea, too!

Chapter 6

Katie dropped the carrot and raced over to Speedy's wheel. She started running as fast as her tiny hamster feet could carry her. The wheel moved round and round. The squeaking got louder and louder.

"Excuse me, class," Mrs. Derkman said finally. "I'm going to have to take Speedy's wheel out of his cage. The noise is making it too hard to learn."

Katie heard Mrs. Derkman's footsteps come near the glass cage. Her tiny hamster heart beat quickly. This was her only chance to get free!

Mrs. Derkman took the lid from the cage.

She reached in with her hand and tried to gently ease the hamster off the wheel.

Before Mrs. Derkman could push her off, Katie leaped out and raced up her teacher's arm. Mrs. Derkman jumped back with surprise as the furry little creature scurried over her bare skin.

Katie looked from Mrs. Derkman's elbow to the floor below. It seemed very far away. But Katie knew she had no choice. She placed her little hamster paws in front of her eyes and jumped!

Thump! Katie landed hard on the cold tile floor. Her hind legs hurt a little. So did her ears. Everyone in the class seemed to be moving and shouting at once.

"Speedy's loose!" Kevin announced.

"Somebody catch him!" Zoe shouted.

"I'll get him," Jeremy volunteered. He got down on his hands and knees.

"No, I'll do it," Ricky Dobbs said. He got down on his hands and knees, too.

"I think I can get him," Mandy yelled.

Suddenly everyone seemed to be grabbing for Katie. Her little hamster body shook with fear. She was lost in a big pile of giant human hands. They were all grabbing for her. Katie couldn't let the kids catch her. They'd put her back in the cage again!

Katie ran toward the front of the room. It seemed more empty there. But as she reached Mrs. Derkman's desk, she caught a whiff of human. Whoever was standing there was covered in kid smells—spilled orange juice, crumbs, and waxy crayons.

Suddenly, the boy by the desk shrieked. "Get it away from me! Get this thing away from me!"

Katie would know that voice anywhere. It was George. She couldn't believe it! The big class bully was scared of a tiny little hamster.

Katie couldn't help herself. She ran over to George and brushed up against his leg. Then she climbed right over his shoe.

"AAAAH!" George screamed as he leaped up onto Mrs. Derkman's desk. He stood there, high off the ground, shaking. "Get it! Somebody catch that furball!" he screamed.

Katie laughed to herself. The class bully had been bullied—by a tiny little hamster. Deep down, Katie knew she'd been pretty mean. Her parents had always told her that two wrongs don't make a right, but Katie couldn't help feeling just a little bit happy at hearing George screaming in fear.

Just then, the classroom door opened.

Mr. Kane, the principal, was standing at the door. "What's going on in here?" he asked.

"Our hamster is loose," Suzanne explained quickly.

"There he goes!" Miriam added, as Katie ran right between Mr. Kane's legs and out the door.

"Hang on, Speedy!" Kevin cried out. "We'll save you!"

Chapter 7

"Not so fast, Kevin," Mr. Kane said. "I can't have a whole third-grade class running around the school."

"But we have to find Speedy," Kevin argued.

"Right now you have to go to gym class," Mrs. Derkman interrupted. "I'm sure Speedy will turn up."

"But Mrs. Derkman," Jeremy pleaded. "He could get stuck in a wall or something."

Mrs. Derkman sighed. "I'm sure he'll be fine, Jeremy. Now, class, let's line up. We're already late."

Katie raced down the hall as quickly as her little legs could take her. She was looking for someplace where she could be safe.

As she turned the corner, Katie found herself in a small empty room. What a relief! There was no one here to chase her. She stood on her hind legs and began to clean her front paws with her little pink tongue.

Just then, Katie heard footsteps coming into the room. She froze in place as someone turned on a light.

"Man, Brennan, you are such a chicken!" Katie recognized Ricky's voice. "I didn't think you would be afraid of a tiny hamster."

"I'm not," George answered him.

"So how come you were screaming like that?" Ricky continued.

"How come your face is like that?" George argued back.

It wasn't much of an answer, but it sure shut Ricky up. "I'm not afraid of anything," George continued.

Katie sniffed at the air. The room was beginning to smell like old sneakers and dirty socks.

"Do you think Coach G. will make us play kickball again?" Kevin asked. "I hate that game."

"Well, we'd better hurry up and get out there. Coach gets mad when we take too long in the locker room," Jeremy said.

Katie's eyes grew wide. Oh no! She was in the boys' locker room . . . while the boys were getting dressed for gym! This was so embarrassing!

Katie had to find a good hiding place.

Someplace where the boys couldn't see her.

Someplace where she couldn't see anything she wasn't supposed to see!

Quickly, Katie leaped into the nearest small hole. She landed in some sort of strange, soft cave. She crept inside as far as she could go. Then she sat very, very still.

The inside of the cave was moist and

stinky. It smelled like sweaty feet. But at least
it was dark and quiet. No one would find her
here.

Suddenly, Katie felt someone
lift her hiding place right
off the floor. Katie peeked
out and looked up. A
giant, stinky gym
sock was coming
right at her!

Yikes!

Katie's safe
cave was actually someone's sneaker. And
whoever the sneaker belonged to was about to
crush her with his big, smelly foot!

Katie had to escape from her sneaker cave.
She ran toward the opening, and leaped out
onto the floor.

"AAAAHHHH!" George screamed as he
dropped his sneaker. "There's a mouse in my
shoe!" He leaped up on a bench. "Get it out of
here!"

"That's no mouse," Ricky yelled. "That's Speedy!"

"We've got to get him," Manny Gonzalez shouted.

But Katie wasn't about to be caught in the boys' locker room. She ran for the door.

The boys' screams were way in the distance by the time Katie felt safe enough to stop running. She hid behind a trash can and stood very, very still. She was trying to hear if anyone was coming after her. Luckily, the hallway was silent.

Suddenly a wind began to blow. Katie lifted her little hamster nose and tried to sniff at the breeze. She didn't smell anything unusual— just the ammonia that the janitor, Mr. Peterson, used to clean the floor. She couldn't smell any flowers, trees, or even car fumes coming from outside the school. In fact, there didn't seem to be a window open anywhere.

Still, the wind was definitely blowing. Katie could feel it whipping through her thick, orange fur. It swirled all around her like a tornado . . . exactly as it had just before Katie had turned into a hamster!

Oh no! Katie thought. *What's happening to me now?*

Chapter 8

Finally, the magical wind stopped blowing. But Katie was afraid to open her eyes. She'd already been turned into a hamster. What if this time she were something even worse— like an ant or something?

Slowly, Katie cracked open one eye. She raised her hands to her face. No fur. Good. And she had fingers—five of them on each hand. She looked at her nails. They were filed short. A few of them still showed a few chips of leftover glow-in-the-dark glitter nail polish. These were definitely her hands.

Was it possible? Had she turned back into herself?

Quickly, Katie ran into the girls' room and looked in the mirror. An eight-year-old girl with red hair, green eyes, and a line of freckles across her nose looked back at her. It was true! Katie was back!

Out of the corner of her eye, Katie saw a small orange ball of fluff rush past her into

one of the bathroom stalls. Speedy! The real Speedy was really on the loose. Quickly she ran into the stall. She found Speedy hiding behind the toilet. He seemed frightened and confused.

Katie scooped the hamster up and held him in her hands. "It's okay, little guy," she told him quietly. "Everything's back to normal now."

As Katie walked back to the gym, the voices of her friends became louder. They were all complaining because Coach G. and Mrs. Derkman wouldn't let them chase after Speedy. Katie grinned as she opened the gym door. She would be a hero for bringing the hamster back.

"Were you guys looking for this?" she asked as she walked in the door.

"Katie, where'd you find him?" Suzanne shouted from the other side of the room.

"Oh, we just sort of ran into each other in the girls' room," Katie replied.

"Boy, it was a good thing you were late today," Kevin told her. "Otherwise Speedy might have been gone forever."

"It's never a good thing to be late for school, Kevin," Mrs. Derkman reminded him. "But I am glad you found the hamster, Katie. Now, please put take him back to the classroom and put him in his cage. And make sure the lid is on tightly."

Katie did as she was told. She pet Speedy gently as she placed him down on his cage floor. Then she handed him a treat bar.

"You deserve this," she whispered quietly. "We worked really hard this morning."

Speedy slept for the rest of the morning. Katie spent the time trying to keep her mind on her lessons. But it was hard for her to think about anything other than her adventure. After all, how often does an eight-year-old girl turn into a hamster?

Katie wished she could tell Jeremy and Suzanne all about what had happened to her. But she knew they would never believe her. She wouldn't believe it either if it hadn't happened to her.

This was one secret Katie would have to keep to herself.

"Boy, did you pick the wrong morning to be late," Jeremy told Katie as they walked out onto the playground after lunch. "It was so weird. Speedy was out of his mind. I'd never seen him like that!"

"I'd never seen George like that either," Suzanne giggled. "I can't believe you missed it, Katie. He was terrified of a little hamster. What a wimp!"

"I can't believe we were ever scared of

George," Miriam agreed.

"I was never afraid of him," Kevin argued.

Jeremy rolled his eyes. "So how come you walk three blocks out of your way to get to school—just so you don't have to pass his house on the way?"

Kevin blushed.

The kids looked over at George. He was sitting on a bench all by himself. He didn't look mean anymore. He just looked lonely.

"Hey, George!" Manny Gonzalez called out. "Why did the hamster cross the road?"

George didn't answer. He obviously didn't want to talk about hamsters.

"Because it was the chicken's day off!" Manny finished off his own joke. Then he waited for George to say something mean to him.

But George didn't say anything. He just scowled and turned away. For the first time, the other kids were doing the teasing. George didn't like that at all.

"Well, I guess we don't have to be afraid of George anymore," Jeremy said to the others.

Suzanne nodded. "We have Speedy to thank for that."

Katie smiled to herself. She knew that class 3A actually had her to thank for stopping George's bullying. She was a real hero.

Chapter 9

Katie was in a great mood when she got home that afternoon. Pepper met her at the steps. Katie bent down and gave her cocker spaniel a huge hug.

Pepper licked her on the nose.

"Well, I'm glad to see you're happy again," Katie's mother said as she came out of the house with two glasses of pink lemonade. "You just weren't yourself this morning."

Katie laughed. Her mother didn't know the half of it.

"So, did anything exciting happen at school today?" her mother asked.

Katie almost choked on her lemonade. It

was only the most exciting—and scary—day of her whole life! But Katie couldn't tell her mother that. Instead she said, "Our hamster got loose, and I caught him!"

"Good for you!" her mother said. Then she shuddered. "I can't imagine having a hamster running loose around a classroom. I don't really like little rodents like that."

"Oh, you'd like Speedy, Mom. I know you would." Katie finished off her drink.

"So, what do you want to do this afternoon?" Katie's mom asked as she sipped slowly at her drink. "You want to come inside and have some cookies before you start your homework?"

Katie shook her head. "We don't have a whole lot of homework today. Just a current events worksheet. So can Pepper and I go for a walk?"

"I don't see why not," her mother said. "You can do the worksheet after dinner. I'll put the newspaper up in your room."

Katie handed her mom the empty glass and jumped up.

"Come on, Pepper!" she called out. "Let's walk!"

Katie never thought she'd be so happy just to walk around on two legs. But it felt great to stand straight and tall. She loved being able to run wherever she wanted, not just on some silly, squeaky wheel. Katie did a big cartwheel, right in the middle of the sidewalk.

Unfortunately, Katie was not very good at cartwheels. Instead of landing on her feet, she landed—*splat*—right on her rear end.

57

As Katie stood up, she noticed a boy about her age sitting alone on his front porch. He was wearing dark sunglasses and a baseball hat. At first she didn't recognize him. Then the boy called out, "You okay?"

It was George Brennan. A nervous feeling came over Katie. Was George going to make fun of her for falling down?

"I said, are you okay?"

Katie stood up and brushed off her jeans. "Yeah, I'm fine. Thanks." She looked at George. He seemed more embarrassed than she was. He seemed kind of sad, too.

For the first time, Katie felt a little sorry for George. At least when George had made fun of her for falling in the mud, she'd had friends to cheer her up. George had no one.

"Is this your house?" she asked him nervously.

"No, I just like to sit on other people's porches," George snapped back, making a nasty joke. "Of course it's my house."

Katie turned and began to walk away. If George was going to be mean, she wasn't going to talk to him.

"Hey, is that your dog?" George called after her.

Katie stopped walking. She turned around and smiled. "No, I just like hanging out with other people's dogs," she joked back. "Of course he's my dog."

George smiled—a little bit. "Good one," he admitted.

Katie smiled back. "His name's Pepper. You want to pet him? Or are you afraid of dogs, too?"

George blushed. "Never mind."

Katie felt bad. She hadn't been teasing. She really didn't know if George had a problem with all animals, or just hamsters.

"No, I mean it," she assured him. "If you were afraid of dogs, it wouldn't be such a bad thing. A lot of people are afraid dogs will bite or something. But Pepper wouldn't do that."

"I'm not afraid of dogs," George told her. "I'm not even afraid of hamsters. This morning I was just sort of goofing on all the kids who were afraid of Speedy. You weren't there. You should have seen them all crying and screaming and stuff."

Katie knew that was a lie. None of the other kids were afraid of Speedy. They were all trying to catch the hamster. The only kid crying and jumping on chairs was George.

But Katie didn't tell George that. He'd only wonder how she knew what was going on in the classroom, since the whole class thought she was late for school today. Besides, George must have felt really embarrassed about being afraid of hamsters. Why else would he lie about it?

"Oh, I guess everyone else got it wrong," Katie told him, trying to be nice.

"I guess," George mumbled.

"So, you want to pet my dog then?" Katie asked.

"Okay," George said quietly.

Katie walked Pepper up toward George's house. George reached his hand out slowly. It was obvious that he was nervous around dogs, too, but he wasn't going to admit it to Katie. Pepper sat on his hind legs and lifted his head. When George gave Pepper a little pat, the dog licked George's hand. George wrinkled up his nose. He wasn't used to dog kisses.

"He's a pretty cool dog," George admitted.

"Thanks," Katie replied, sitting down next to George. "You know, it's okay to be afraid of something."

George frowned. "Oh yeah, right. So what are you afraid of?"

"I *was* afraid of you—at least until today," Katie admitted.

George smiled. He seemed almost proud of the fact that Katie had been scared of him.

"So you're not afraid of me anymore, huh?" he asked her finally.

Katie shook her head. "Nope."

"I guess none of the kids are scared of me after today," George moaned.

"Why would you want us to be scared of you?" Katie asked.

George shrugged. "Just because."

"I don't know why you have to make mean jokes all the time," Katie said.

"I make jokes so that people will laugh," George told her. "I'd rather have people laugh

at my jokes than laugh at me."

"Why do you think people will laugh at you?" Katie asked him.

George looked at her and rolled his eyes. "Are you kidding? I'm the new kid. Everyone makes fun of the new kid. They laugh at the way the new kid talks, and the clothes the new kid wears. This is the third school I've been to since kindergarten. My dad has had to switch jobs three times. But you know what? After today, I wish my family could move again."

"Don't say that!" Katie exclaimed. "Don't make wishes you don't really mean. You never know when they'll come true."

"But I'm miserable here," George said. "All the kids hate me. And now they won't even laugh at my jokes."

Katie thought about that for a minute. Then she had an idea. "Don't you know any jokes that aren't mean?" Katie asked George. "You can still make kids laugh without making them feel bad."

"I don't know," George answered. "I've never thought about jokes that weren't mean."

"I have a bunch of joke books at my house. Do you want to come over and look at some of them? You can try the jokes out on the kids at school tomorrow."

George didn't say anything at first. Then he looked sort of embarrassed. "I'm sorry I kept calling you Katie Kazoo," he said finally.

Katie grinned. "It's okay. I kind of like it, actually."

"You do?" George asked.

Katie nodded. "It's a pretty cool nickname. It's the kind of name Suzanne would give herself—if she could."

George looked at Katie. "How come you're being nice to me?" he demanded.

Katie shrugged. "I guess because you're being nice to me," she said simply.

Chapter 10

The next morning Katie was up and dressed before her parents awoke. She wanted to be sure to get to school before George did. Katie had a feeling that the other kids were going to make fun of George for being afraid of Speedy. If they did, he might be mean right back to them. Then he would never make friends at school.

Katie really wanted to help George. They had spent a lot of time laughing at joke books together yesterday afternoon. George was really an okay kid. Katie hoped the other kids could see that side of him.

Besides, Katie figured that if George made

friends with the kids at school, he wouldn't want to make fun of them. School would be a lot more fun if everybody wasn't always afraid that George would say something mean to them. So, by helping George, Katie was helping all the other kids, too.

If her plan worked, Katie would be a hero two days in a row!

Katie got to the schoolyard ten minutes early. She sat down on a bench and waited for her friends—and George—to arrive.

"You're here early," Suzanne said a few minutes later, plopping down onto the bench beside Katie.

The key chains on Suzanne's backpack jingled and jangled as the pack hit the ground. Suzanne had a stretchy-alien key chain, a Slinky dog key chain, a key chain that looked like a Barbie doll, and key chains from Vermont, Texas, and California. She even had a key chain with a mirror on it.

Katie only had two key chains on her back-pack. One was a photo frame with a picture of Pepper in it. The other one was a little rubber monkey that bounced up and down when you shook it.

"Are you trying to make up for being late yesterday?" Suzanne asked.

Katie shook her head. "I'm just waiting."

"For what?"

Katie shrugged. "Oh, nothing."

laughing—really hard. He was totally cracking up. The other kids looked at him in amazement.

Jeremy stared back at them. "What?" he asked. "It was funny."

"Thanks," George said. He sounded a little happier now.

"Tell another one," Katie urged.

"Okay," George agreed. "What's the most important subject a witch learns in school?"

"What?" Katie asked.

"Spelling!" George answered.

Jeremy started laughing again. So did Suzanne. Suddenly all the kids were giggling at George's joke.

"That was a good one," Kevin said. "Got any more jokes?"

George's face broke into a smile. A real, happy smile, not the mean smile he usually had on his face. "Sure, I've got a million of 'em." He looked around at the other kids. "Why didn't the skeleton do well in school?"

"Why?" Suzanne asked.

"Because his heart wasn't in it!" George said.

Everyone started laughing all over again.

"Wait, wait! Here's another one!" George announced. "What's the hardest part about taking a test?"

"What?" asked Mandy.

"The answers!" George told her.

George was on a roll. He couldn't stop telling jokes. That was a good thing, since the kids didn't want him to stop. "What table doesn't have any legs?" he asked Jeremy.

Jeremy thought for a minute, but he couldn't guess. "I don't know," he said finally.

"A multiplication table!" George shouted out.

Once again the kids all started giggling.

Just then, Mrs. Derkman blew her whistle. "Line up, class 3A!" she called out. The kids ran to line up. Katie found herself standing right in front of George. Just one day ago, that would have been an awful place to stand.

But now, Katie didn't mind standing near George at all.

"Hey, Katie Kazoo, what do you have for lunch?" George whispered into Katie's ear.

"I'm going to buy something from the cafeteria," she whispered back. "My mom gave me lunch money today."

"I have peanut butter and Marshmallow Fluff," George said. "My mom hardly ever gives me lunch money."

"You're lucky," Katie said. "The food in the cafeteria stinks. I'd much rather have peanut butter and Marshmallow Fluff."

"We could sit together in the cafeteria and share," George suggested. "I'll give you half of my sandwich if you'll give me half of your dessert."

Katie grinned. "It's a deal!"

As class 3A walked toward the school building, Katie felt a cool breeze blow through her hair. She got a scared feeling in the pit of her stomach. Was this the same wind that had turned her into a hamster yesterday? What was going to happen to her now?

Then Katie noticed that everyone else's hair was blowing around too. This wasn't some sort of magic wind. It was just a normal, everyday breeze—the kind that cools you down without turning you into someone else.

Still, Katie had a feeling she hadn't seen the last of the magic wind. It was bound to start blowing again sometime. So the only question was . . . who was she going to turn into next?

Fun Facts About Hamsters!

If you're like Katie and have a hamster in your classroom, here are some fun facts about your furry friend.

Did you know that:

Hamsters need glasses? Hamsters are very near-sighted. Depending on the breed, they can usually see only a few inches or a few feet in front of themselves.

Hamster teeth never stop growing? They just keep getting longer and longer—unless you give your hamster something to gnaw on, like a wooden chew stick. When hamsters chew, they keep their teeth short and healthy.

Hamsters need lots of exercise? In the wild, hamsters may travel several miles a night in search of food. Hamsters that are kept as pets need the same amount of exercise, which is why they run on their wheels.

Hamsters squeak to get your attention?
Hamsters usually make squeaking noises
when they want more food or attention.

Hamsters sometimes eat their poop? As
gross as it may sound, hamsters sometimes do
just that. Their digestive systems are different
than ours. Some hamster poop contains cer-
tain nutrients that the hamster needs.

Hamsters don't need shampoo? All hamsters know how to clean themselves. They
don't need fancy sponges and shampoo to do
it either. Hamsters groom themselves by licking
their coat at the back and the front. They also
lick their paws and then rub their paws over
their face and behind their ears. They do that
because they can't actually lick their faces.

Some hamsters take baths in dry sand?
Hamsters love rolling around in sand. The
sand takes some of the grease off of their
skin. That makes them feel more comfortable.
If you have a hamster, you might want to put
a dish of sand in the cage for the hamster to
roll around in.

Katie Kazoo, SWITCHEROO

Out to Lunch

For The Breakfast Club:
Rena, Patrice, Marcy, and Vivian.
—N.K.

Text copyright © 2002 by Nancy Krulik. Illustrations copyright © 2002
by John & Wendy. All rights reserved. Published by Grosset & Dunlap,
a division of Penguin Young Readers Group, 345 Hudson Street,
New York, New York 10014. GROSSET & DUNLAP is a trademark
of Penguin Random House LLC.
Manufactured in China

Library of Congress Control Number: 2002102953

10 9 8 7 6 5 4 3 2 1

Proprietary ISBN 978-1-101-95129-3
Part of Boxed Set, ISBN 978-1-101-95128-6

Katie Kazoo, SWITCHEROO

Out to Lunch

by Nancy Krulik • illustrated by John & Wendy

Grosset & Dunlap

Chapter 1

"How many tomatoes are you going to eat?" Katie Carew asked her friend Kevin Camilleri as she plopped down into the seat across from him in the school cafeteria. Kevin had opened his lunch box. Inside were all sorts of tomatoes—tiny grape tomatoes; small, round cherry tomatoes; oval-shaped plum tomatoes; and a big plastic bag filled with sliced tomatoes. And for dessert, he had a bag of tomato-flavored chips.

Kevin picked up one of the oval-shaped tomatoes and bit into it like an apple. "I could probably eat about a million of these. I love tomatoes!"

All the kids at the table laughed. They knew that Kevin had been a tomato freak since kindergarten. Back then they had even nicknamed him Tomato Man.

"You've never met a tomato you didn't like, right, Kevin?" Katie teased.

"That's not true," Kevin said. "I'd never eat a tomato from the school salad bar."

The kids at the table agreed. The vegetables at the salad bar were pretty gross.

"Hey, how do you stop a rotten tomato from smelling?" George Brennan asked, dropping his tray down next to Katie. George loved jokes and riddles. He told them all the time.

"How?" Kevin asked him.

"Hold its nose!" George answered. He began laughing hysterically. He turned to Katie. "Good one, huh, Katie Kazoo?"

Katie giggled. She loved George's jokes. She didn't even mind when he called her Katie Kazoo. She thought the nickname sounded sort of cool! She'd even tried signing

Katie Kazoo on her schoolwork—until her teacher, Mrs. Derkman, made her write her real name on her papers.

"Whoops," Katie knocked her spoon off the table when she laughed. "Hold my place George," she told him. "I'll be right back."

Katie got up from the table and walked over to the lunch counter. "May I have a spoon?" she asked the lunch lady.

"Didn't you get one already?" the lunch lady answered in a very grouchy voice.

"I dropped it," Katie explained.

"Tough toenails," the lunch lady told her. "One spoon per customer."

"But how am I going to eat my pudding?"

The lunch lady rolled her eyes. "Use your hands. Or better yet, don't eat it at all. I wouldn't."

The lunch lady hadn't been very nice. But she was probably right. The pudding looked disgusting, and it smelled worse. Katie *was* better off not eating it.

Katie went back to the lunch table. She sat down and looked at her apple. If she ate around the rotten spot, it might be okay.

"Got room over here for me?" Suzanne Lock asked.

Katie scooted over to make room for her best friend. Suzanne put down her cafeteria tray and sat beside Katie.

"I thought you were sitting at the other

table with Jeremy," Katie said. She looked over at the long table in the corner, where Jeremy Fox sat with two boys from the other third grade class. Katie had known Jeremy and Suzanne practically since they were babies. Jeremy and Suzanne were pals, but they didn't think of each other as best friends. Katie considered both of them her best friends, though.

"Jeremy's looking at some dumb baseball book," Suzanne explained. "It's soooo boring!"

She placed her spoon into her bowl of alphabet soup and fished around. A moment later, she lifted the spoon and smiled. "Look! I spelled rat!"

Katie looked onto Suzanne's spoon. Sure enough, the letters R, A, and T were sitting in a sea of light orange water.

Katie giggled.

Suzanne put the spoon in her mouth and

made a funny face. "Even a rat wouldn't eat this stuff," she said. "It's terrible—just water with food coloring! It has no flavor at all."

Katie nodded. "I know what you mean. The food in this cafeteria is awful, and almost everything is made with some sort of meat. All I ever get to eat for lunch is a stale bagel and Jell-O."

"Oh, come on, Katie. Sometimes they serve gloppy, overcooked macaroni and cheese and old carrot sticks," Suzanne teased. "You can eat that."

"Yuck!" Katie exclaimed.

"That's what you get for being a vegetarian." Kevin told Katie.

"Did you hear the one about the guy with carrot sticks stuck in his ears?" George interrupted.

Katie shook her head. "No."

"That's okay," George shrugged. "He didn't hear it either!"

As George laughed at his own joke,

Suzanne frowned. "That one was really bad, George," she said. She turned back to Katie. "The fried chicken nuggets aren't too bad, and they serve those a lot. I don't know why you won't even eat a piece of chicken once in a while."

"I told you, I won't eat anything that had a face," Katie explained.

"But chickens have *ugly* faces," Kevin pointed out.

"I won't eat any animals," Katie insisted. "Of course, that doesn't leave me with many choices in the cafeteria."

"Why don't you ask your mom to pack your lunches?" Miriam Chan suggested as she took a bite of a turkey sandwich her mother had packed.

"She doesn't have time," Katie explained. "On the days she opens the store, she leaves for work at the same time I leave for school. Our house is crazy in the mornings." Katie's mom worked part time at The Book Nook, a small bookstore in the Cherrydale Mall.

"Well, I'm glad my mom packs my lunch," Kevin said. "That way, I don't ever have to face the *Lunch Lady*!" He made a scary face.

"You know what happened to me today?" Suzanne said. "I asked the lunch lady if I could have a banana that wasn't totally brown and mushy. You know what she told me? She said, 'If you want fresh fruit, get it from home. Brown mushy bananas are what's on the cafeteria menu today.' "

"She's such a grump!" Kevin said.

"You'd be grumpy too if you had to dish out smelly, disgusting food all day," Katie told him.

"That's true," Suzanne agreed.

"Speaking of disgusting, look at George!" Zoe Canter exclaimed. "I think I'm gonna throw up!"

Katie looked over at George's tray. It was totally gross. George had mixed his mashed potatoes and vegetable soup together. Then he'd poured his chocolate milk into the mix. Now he was busy stirring in some orange Jell-O.

"Hey, Katie Kazoo, do you dare me to eat this?" he asked her.

Katie made a face. "Yuck!" she exclaimed.

Suzanne stood and picked up her tray. "Come on, Katie," she said. "Let's get out of here before George really does eat that mess."

As Katie and Suzanne headed toward the playground for recess, Suzanne looked back at George and sighed. "Boys can be so dumb," she remarked.

Katie shrugged. Some boys could be pretty

dumb. But other boys were really cool. Like Jeremy. Katie was about to say that, but she stopped herself. Suzanne got mad whenever Katie talked about Jeremy. Suzanne didn't like to think that Katie had two best friends.

"Come on, hurry up!" Suzanne urged Katie. "Let's see if we can get to the hop-scotch game before the fourth-graders do!"

Katie followed her friend out the door.

Katie tossed her stone toward the hop-scotch board. It landed in the middle of the three. Quickly Katie began jumping up and down the board. As she bent down to pick up her stone on the way back, she heard Jeremy's voice over her head.

"You guys want to throw the ball around a little bit?" he asked.

Katie hopped off the board and smiled at Jeremy. "Maybe later," she said. "We're kind of in the middle of a game."

Suzanne gave a deep sigh. "He can see

that, Katie." She turned to Jeremy. "Can't you?"

Jeremy nodded. "I just thought maybe you two would want to play catch, that's all. You said you wanted to work on your aim," he reminded Katie.

"I do," Katie said kindly. "How about after we finish with hopscotch?"

Jeremy shrugged and pushed his glasses further up on his nose. "Sure. See ya later."

As Jeremy walked off, Katie looked at Suzanne. "You sounded kind of angry. Are you mad at Jeremy or something?" she asked.

Suzanne shook her head. "No. I just thought it was really rude of him to try to break up our game."

Katie nodded. "I guess we could have asked him if he wanted to play with us instead."

"He wouldn't have wanted to play hop-scotch," Suzanne told Katie. "None of the boys play hopscotch anymore."

Katie shrugged. Suzanne was probably

right. But they could have asked Jeremy to play anyway, just to be nice.

Just then Mandy Banks came strolling over. Miriam and Zoe were right behind her. They were each carrying flat, smooth stones— perfect for hopscotch.

"Can we play with you?" Mandy asked.

Suzanne smiled brightly. "Sure. You're right after Katie, Mandy. Then Zoe, then Miriam. This game is for third-grade girls only . . . right Katie?"

Katie didn't answer. She didn't like it when games were just for girls or just for boys. She was much happier when everybody got to play. Katie tucked her red hair behind her ears. Then she reached out and tossed her stone toward the square with the four in it. The small rock soared right over the box, and landed on the eight instead.

"Your turn, Mandy," Suzanne called out cheerfully.

Chapter 2

Classroom 3A was a wild place after lunch.

"Look out, incoming plane," George shouted as he threw a paper airplane toward Kevin.

Kevin laughed. "Back at ya!" He tossed the plane back to George.

Suzanne ducked as the paper plane shot over her head. "Hey! Watch it!" she shouted at Kevin.

"That's enough now," Mrs. Derkman told the class. "Recess is over. Please take out your writer's notebooks. We're going to work on our biographies."

Katie smiled. She loved writing biographies. Right now she was working on one about her dog, Pepper. Katie had taken care of him since he was a puppy. Pepper was like a brother to her—even better because Pepper didn't argue or ask to share her toys.

Squeak. Squeak. Squeak. Katie looked over toward the class hamster's cage. Boy, did Speedy's wheel need oiling.

Mrs. Derkman must have heard the squeaking, too, because she said, "Oh, class, before I forget—the classroom floors are being cleaned this weekend. I will need someone to take Speedy home. If you're interested, bring me a note from your parents saying it's okay."

Katie knew she couldn't even think about bringing Speedy home for the weekend—not with Pepper living there. Dogs and hamsters didn't always get along so well.

Still, Katie really wished she could take Speedy home. She cared about him more than anyone else in the whole class. Maybe that was because Katie was the only one in the class who had actually been Speedy.

It was true! Katie had actually turned into the class hamster for a whole morning!

It happened a few weeks ago. After a really, really bad day, Katie had made the mistake of wishing she could be anyone but herself.

There must have been some sort of shooting star flying through the sky at the very moment Katie had made the wish, because it had come true. (And everyone knows when you make a wish on a shooting star, it comes true!) The only thing was, instead of turning into some*one* else, Katie had turned into some*thing* else—Speedy!

Katie shivered a little as she remembered being a hamster. It was really scary. She thought she'd be stuck in that tiny, smelly glass cage forever. But eventually she'd gotten loose. And luckily, once she was free, Katie had somehow turned back into herself.

Katie didn't understand how any of it had happened. All she knew was that she was really glad to be an eight-year-old girl again.

Ever since she'd spent time in Speedy's body, Katie had taken great care of the little hamster. She always made sure his water bowl was full, gave him plenty of chew sticks, and brought him fresh carrots from home.

Of course, Katie had never told anyone about turning into Speedy. She didn't think they would believe her. She wouldn't have believed it if it hadn't happened to her.

"Hey, Katie Kazoo, if I took Speedy home, you know what I would do with him?" George whispered from the desk next to Katie's.

"What?" Katie whispered back.

"Keep him in the refrigerator," George answered.

Katie looked at George with surprise. "Why would you do that?"

"To keep him from getting spoiled," George told her. "Nobody likes a spoiled hamster!"

Katie smiled and sighed. She knew George was only joking. George would never take Speedy home. He was afraid of hamsters!

As soon as the school bell rang, Katie packed up her backpack and hurried toward the door. She couldn't wait to get out of the school. It had been a very long afternoon.

Jeremy and Katie met up on the school's front steps. "I'm definitely asking my mother if I can take Speedy home," he announced.

Katie smiled. She knew how badly Jeremy wanted a pet. His mother kept saying she was waiting to see if he was responsible enough to care for one. "Great!" Katie exclaimed. "Once your mom sees how you feed Speedy, give him water, and change the dirty litter in his cage, she'll get you your own pet for sure."

"I have to change the litter?" Jeremy asked, scrunching up his nose.

"Of course," Katie told him. "Otherwise, it starts to stink!"

Before Jeremy could answer, Suzanne

came bounding down the steps toward them. "I'm so excited!" she announced.

"How come?" Katie asked her.

" 'Cause I'm going to ask my mom to let me bring Speedy home this weekend. It'll be so much fun to have him there. I'm going to build him a whole hamster playground. I can use toilet paper tubes, egg cartons, and . . . "

"Wait a minute," Jeremy interrupted her. "*You're* not bringing Speedy home."

"Why not?" Suzanne asked.

"Because *I'm* bringing him home," he told her.

"Are not!" Suzanne exclaimed.

"Am, too!" Jeremy shouted back.

"Yeah, who says?" Suzanne demanded.

"I do!" Jeremy yelled.

Suzanne looked straight at Katie. "Which one of us do *you* think Speedy should go home with?" she asked.

Katie wasn't sure what to say. As she looked from Jeremy to Suzanne, she wasn't

sure who Speedy would be happier with.
Jeremy promised he would take good care of
Speedy, but Katie knew Jeremy had a Little
League game on Saturday. What if he was so
busy thinking about baseball that he forgot to
feed Speedy?

On the other hand, Suzanne might not be

able to take care of Speedy very well, either. Suzanne's mom had just had a new baby. Now that little Heather had arrived, things were really crazy at Suzanne's house. People were always stopping by to see the new baby, and everyone was busy running around, changing diapers and heating up bottles. What if someone knocked the lid off of Speedy's cage by accident? The hamster would be long gone before anyone in her house even realized he'd escaped.

"Come on, Katie, who do you think should get to take Speedy home?" Suzanne asked Katie again.

Katie had a sick feeling in her stomach. No matter what she said, somebody would be mad at her. So, instead of making a decision, Katie walked away. "I have to get home and feed Pepper," she told her friends quickly. "Talk to you later."

Chapter 3

The next day there was trouble in room 3A. Jeremy and Suzanne both came to school with notes from their parents saying they could bring Speedy home for the weekend. Katie hoped that Mrs. Derkman would just pick one kid or the other to take the hamster. But that's not what the teacher decided to do.

"You two will have to work this out between you," Mrs. Derkman told Jeremy and Suzanne. "You have until the end of the week to tell me what you decide."

Katie thought that was just about the most terrible thing her teacher could have done. Neither Jeremy nor Suzanne was going to give in. It didn't seem like her friends even cared about taking care of Speedy anymore. All they cared about was winning.

The whole class was caught up in the war between Suzanne and Jeremy. All the boys were siding with Jeremy. The girls were all on Suzanne's side—except Katie. She didn't know whose side to be on. Jeremy and Suzanne were both her best friends.

Unfortunately, Jeremy and Suzanne weren't friends with each other anymore.

"You're going to sit with me, aren't you, Katie?" Suzanne asked as class 3A walked into the cafeteria.

"Who says she's gonna sit with you?" Jeremy interrupted. "She was my friend before she ever met you."

Suzanne rolled her eyes. "That's just because your moms knew each other when they were kids," she explained. "You guys probably wouldn't have become friends if it weren't for that."

George pulled a bag of potato chips from his lunch bag. "Do you know why best friends are like potatoes?" he asked jokingly.

"No, why?" Katie said.

"Because they're always there when the *chips* are down!" George started to laugh. "Get it?"

Katie smiled. She was glad George was trying to make everyone laugh. "That was funny," she told him.

Suzanne put her arm around Katie. "Katie's like that," she told the others. "She's always on *my* side."

Jeremy moved closer toward Katie. "No, she's always on my side," he argued.

Katie could feel the tears starting to build

up in her eyes. This just wasn't fair. "Look, you guys, I like both of you. I don't want to have to choose. I wish I could just cut myself in half," she said.

George started to laugh.

"What's so funny about that?" Katie demanded.

"Nothing." George shrugged. "It's just that I was thinking, if you cut your left side off, you'd be *all right*." He laughed again.

But for once Katie didn't laugh with him. She felt like nothing was going to be alright ever again. Quickly she turned and ran back into the hall. "I have to go to the bathroom," she mumbled as she darted away.

Katie walked into the girls' room and looked around. There was no one else there. It was nice to be alone. Maybe she could just stay in the bathroom until lunch was over. That way she could keep away from Suzanne, Jeremy, and everyone else in her class.

Katie looked at her watch. It was 12:05. Lunch was over at 1:00. That meant she would have to stay in the girls' room for fifty-five minutes. That was a very long time. What could she do in the bathroom for fifty-five minutes? Katie looked at her watch again. Make that fifty-four minutes. The hands on her watch had just moved to 12:06.

Well, for starters, she could wash her face and hands. Katie turned on the water and held her hands under the faucet.

Suddenly Katie felt a light wind blowing on her back. She looked up toward the bathroom window. It was closed. So was the door. The wind wasn't coming from outside. It was only blowing in the girls room. Katie gulped as she looked around her. The wind didn't even seem to be blowing anywhere else in the room—just around Katie.

The wind grew stronger and stronger, swirling around her like a tornado. For a minute Katie was sure it was going to lift her right off the ground—like Dorothy in *The Wizard of Oz*. She closed her eyes and grabbed on to the sink, trying to keep herself from flying away.

Katie was really scared. She knew what

trouble this kind of wind could cause. This
wasn't the first time Katie had been trapped
in a strange, magical windstorm. It had happened to her twice before, once when she'd
turned into Speedy, and once when she'd

turned back into herself. This wind could only mean one thing.

Katie Carew was becoming somebody else!

But who?

Or *what*?

After a few seconds, the wind stopped. Everything was quiet—and different. There was a really bad stink in the air. Not a bathroom stink, though. It smelled more like spoiled milk.

"Ow!" Katie yanked her hand from the sink. The cool plaster had suddenly turned really hot.

Where was she?

She slowly opened her eyes and looked nervously toward the mirror. It was time to find out just who she'd changed into.

But as Katie's eyelids fluttered open, she discovered there was no mirror in front of her. There was no sink, either. Katie wasn't even in the bathroom. She was in the cafeteria! She'd just burned her hand on the hot lunch counter.

A really bad smell began to waft up from the table.

"Yuck! What stinks?" Katie said aloud.

She looked down at a stack of disgusting gray hamburgers. Beside the burgers was a pile of old slices of American cheese. One of the slices was covered in green mold. Spoiled cheese and bad hamburgers—Katie felt sick.

Beads of sweat began to form on her forehead. Katie raised her hand to wipe them away. That's when she saw that her hands were much larger than usual—the size of adult hands. She was also wearing clear plastic gloves that made her big hands feel hot and sweaty.

Katie ran her gloved hands over her dress. The dress was mostly white, but there were brown gravy stains all over it. Some of the stains looked like they'd been there for a while. Others looked as though they'd just landed on the dress today.

As Katie reached up to wipe a bead of sweat from her cheek, she felt a sharp pain in her lower back—the kind her mother complained about when she'd spent too many hours standing up at work. Katie's feet really hurt, too. As she looked down, she was amazed to see just how huge her feet had become. Her white shoes looked like big boats on the ends of her legs!

"Excuse me," a fourth-grade boy said to Katie. "Can I have a hot dog and a carton of milk?"

That's when Katie realized what had happened to her.

Katie Carew had turned into Lucille the lunch lady!

Chapter 4

Now what? Katie thought nervously. *I can't do this. I don't want to touch that disgusting meat.*

"What's going on up there?" a sixth-grade girl shouted from the back of the line.

"The lunch lady is so slow," someone else said.

Katie felt like crying. She wasn't used to having kids yell at her. She didn't think being Lucille would be very much fun, but there was nothing she could do about it now.

Katie's only hope was that she had only been stuck inside Speedy's body for a little while. Maybe that's how it would work with

Lucille's body, too. Maybe the magic wind would change Katie back into herself pretty soon. She sure hoped so.

"Come on! Move it!" a sixth-grader shouted.

The kids were getting really mad. Katie wished she could just run away and hide, but there was nowhere for her to go. Katie had no choice. She was Lucille. She had to do what Lucille would do.

She had to serve disgusting food to kids.

"Oh man, not hot dogs again," a fifth-grade boy named Carlos moaned as he stared at a bucket of hot dogs swimming around in boiling water. "We had those yesterday, and three days before that."

"I know how you feel," Katie agreed. "I'm pretty sick of these hounds with Mississippi mud myself. Would you rather have a wimpy instead?"

Hounds with Mississippi mud? Wimpy? Katie was shocked as the weird words left her mouth. She'd never even heard those words before. But somehow she just seemed to know that a hound with Mississippi mud was a hot dog with mustard, and that a wimpy was a hamburger.

It must be some sort of lunchroom code that only lunch ladies know, Katie thought to herself.

"Who are you calling wimpy?" Carlos demanded in an angry voice.

Katie blushed. "Nobody. Wimpy means hamburger."

"Huh?" Carlos asked her.

"Oh, never mind." Katie replied in her best lunch lady voice. "Just move along."

A sixth-grade boy named Malcolm was next in line. "What's the sandwich today?" he asked her.

"Hen fruit," Katie answered. Oops! There was that lunchroom lingo again. "Uh, I mean egg salad," she explained quickly.

"Blech!" Malcolm exclaimed. "I hate egg salad."

Katie sighed. These kids were so mean. They were acting as though she'd cooked the food or something. She knew she had nothing to do with this menu. Lunch ladies weren't chefs. They just served what they were given. It wasn't like she was having a whole lot of fun serving the stuff, either. It was awful standing back there behind the counter, having to stare at rotting fruit and sniffing the scent of boiled hot dogs, overcooked baked beans, and egg salad all day long.

But Katie couldn't argue with Malcolm. She only had to *serve* the food. He actually had to eat it. Katie smiled at him and nodded her head. "I don't like egg salad very much, either," she said as she pointed to the egg salad tray. "Especially *this* egg salad. It's all gloppy. Too much mayonnaise."

"Like always," Malcolm moaned.

"You know where this egg salad belongs?" she asked Malcolm as she picked up a huge scooper full of the yellow-white glop.

"Where?" Malcolm said.

Katie gave him a naughty smile. "In the garbage!" she announced. Then she hurled the egg salad toward the garbage can.

Malcolm stared at her with surprise. He'd never seen Lucille the lunch lady throw food in the garbage before. Nobody had.

Katie watched as the big ball of egg salad soared in the direction of the trash can. Unfortunately, Katie's aim was not very good. The egg salad landed right on top of George's tray.

Katie gulped. *Maybe I should've worked on my throwing with Jeremy yesterday,* she thought to herself. Katie looked nervously at George. She couldn't tell if he was angry or not.

A big smile flashed across George's face. "*Food fight!*" he announced loudly. George shot a big glob of strawberry yogurt right at Kevin. The yogurt landed on a pile of tomato slices inside Kevin's lunch box.

Katie gasped. George shouldn't have done that. He knew how Kevin felt about tomatoes. Kevin was going to be really mad that George had ruined some of them!

A fifth-grader named Stanley was sitting at the next table. He began to laugh. "Looks like your lunch is gone," Stanley told Kevin. "You can't eat it now."

Kevin nodded. "I know. But there are lots of things you can do with a tomato!" He picked up a yogurt-covered tomato slice and flung it right at Stanley. The round slice land-ed in the middle of the fifth-grader's shirt. "Bulls-eye!" Kevin called out excitedly.

After that, it seemed like everyone in
the entire cafeteria started throwing food.
Stanley tossed his jelly sandwich toward the
table where class 3A was sitting. It landed
right on Jeremy's face. Suzanne began to giggle
as Jeremy wiped grape jelly from his glasses.
Jeremy threw a glob of mashed potatoes at
Suzanne. Suzanne rolled a piece of hot dog
bun into a little ball and threw it at Jeremy.

Mandy was so busy watching Suzanne and
Jeremy that she didn't notice a hot dog with
mustard flying towards her. It landed right
on her head. "Oooh! Gross!" she shouted out.
The hot dog slid onto the floor below, but the
mustard stayed in Mandy's hair.

Miriam started giggling. Mandy grinned
and shook her head wildly—splashing yellow
mustard all over Miriam.

Miriam picked up a slice of salami and
threw it at Mandy. Mandy ducked. The salami
landed on Zoe's nose.

George laughed so hard he fell off his

chair and landed on the floor. Zoe picked up her milk and poured it over George's head. George wiped the milk from his eyes, smiled, and licked his lips. "Mmmm!" he exclaimed. "Chocolate. My favorite!"

The kids were going wild! They launched lunchmeat. They flung frankfurters. They heaved hamburgers. Everyone and everything was covered with food. The teachers tried to stop the food fight, but they couldn't. The lunchroom was a mess.

Katie looked up. A canned peach was flying straight at her head. She ducked. The bright orange fruit smacked into the wall behind her and slid toward the floor.

"Look out!" Katie cried as she scooped up two huge handfuls of green Jell-O. "Here comes a Jell-O bomb!" She reached back and threw the glop across the room. The slimy Jell-O flew through the air and landed with a splat . . . *right in the middle of Mr. Kane's forehead.*

Katie had just slimed the school principal!

"Lucille!" Mr. Kane shouted in a very angry voice as he wiped the gooey green stuff from his eyes. "I'll see you in my office in fifteen minutes!"

The entire lunchroom froze. All eyes were on Katie.

Oh no! Katie had totally forgotten she was the lunch lady. She was in big trouble now. "Yes, sir," Katie told the principal, in Lucille's low, grown-up voice.

"As for you students," Mr. Kane continued, "you will be spending the rest of your day cleaning this cafeteria."

Chapter 5

As Katie walked down the hall, she felt a little sick. She had never been called down to the principal's office before—ever. Katie had never done anything bad in school in her whole life. *Until now.*

Katie knew Mr. Kane was going to give her a terrible punishment. She guessed it wasn't going to be something easy, like having to stay after school or writing a long apology note. This was going to be some sort of *grown-up* punishment. After all, Mr. Kane thought he was punishing Lucille the lunch lady, not Katie Carew from class 3A.

Suddenly Katie felt a gentle wind nip at

the back of her neck. She looked behind to see if someone had just opened a door or a window. No one was there.

Katie wasn't surprised when the calm wind began to get stronger. She wasn't shocked when it started blowing wildly around her like a tornado, either. She knew what was about to happen. Katie was going to change into someone else.

"Please, please, please let me turn back into me," she cried to the wind. "I just want to be Katie Carew. Nobody else."

The wind kept blowing harder and harder. Katie closed her eyes and held on tight to one of the lockers.

After a few minutes, the tornado stopped. The wind just disappeared, leaving no marks or traces in the hall. Not even one piece of paper was out of place. Slowly, Katie opened her eyes and looked down. Lucille's gravy-stained white dress was gone. Black jeans and a white sweater had taken its place. Those were the clothes Katie had worn to school that morning. Katie checked her reflection in a nearby classroom window. An eight-year-old girl with red hair, green eyes, and a line of

freckles on her nose looked back at her from the glass.

Katie Carew was back!

As Katie smiled at her reflection, she heard Mr. Kane's voice coming from his office.

"Lucille! I don't know what's gotten into you!" the principal yelled.

"I don't know what's gotten into me, either, Mr. Kane," Lucille said. "Come to think of it, I don't even know how I wound up here in your office."

Katie was surprised to hear the lunch lady's voice. How had she gotten to Mr. Kane's office so quickly? Did she know what had happened in the cafeteria? Did she remember that Katie had been inside her body?

"One minute, I'm in the cafeteria, handing out food. The next minute I'm standing here," Lucille continued. "I can't really remember anything in between."

"*Handing out food?*" Mr. Kane demanded. "Is that what you call slinging Jell-O across the cafeteria?"

"No sir," Lucille answered.

"Are you saying you *didn't* throw food in the cafeteria?" Mr. Kane asked her.

"No. I think I did throw food."

"You *think* you threw food?" Mr. Kane repeated.

Lucille shrugged. "I'm pretty sure I did . . . I think. I don't know. You saw me throw it, right?"

Mr. Kane nodded.

"So I must have," Lucille continued. "It's all very strange. I guess I just wasn't myself today."

"I can't understand what would make you waste perfectly good food," Mr. Kane continued.

"Well, I wouldn't call it 'perfectly good food,' " Lucille argued. "It's terrible food. We need to give those kids fresh fruits and vegetables, and there need to be more choices on the menu. I can understand why the kids treated the food like garbage. It *is* garbage. Now if I were in charge . . . "

That made Mr. Kane more angry than ever. "Well, you're not in charge," he told Lucille in a furious voice. "In fact, as of right now, you don't even work here anymore!"

Wow! Lucille had been fired! Now Katie felt really guilty. The food fight wasn't Lucille's fault. Katie wished she could run into Mr. Kane's office and tell him that it was her fault, but she knew the principal wouldn't believe her. A girl who turned into a lunch lady when a magical wind blew on her? Katie shook her head. Nobody would ever believe a story like that.

Quickly, Katie hurried back to the cafeteria. The least she could do was help the other kids clean up.

Chapter 6

That afternoon, Katie sat in her room with the door closed. She didn't feel very much like going out to play. Even if she did feel like playing, there'd be no one to play with. Most of the kids from school were grounded because they'd been in the food fight.

Still, Katie bet that none of the other kids felt as bad as she did. All they had lost was an afternoon of TV or a trip to the playground. Katie had made Lucille lose her job.

Katie began to cry. As soon as he saw Katie's tears, Pepper jumped up on the bed and sat beside her. He stuck out his big, red tongue and licked her face. But even a big, sloppy, wet, dog-kiss couldn't cheer up Katie. She used the back of her hand to wipe Pepper's slobber from her cheek. Pepper lifted his back paw and scratched at his floppy ear.

Just then there was a knock at the door. "Katie, Suzanne is on the phone," her mother said.

Katie walked downstairs to the kitchen and picked up the phone. "Hi, Suzanne," she said.

"Hey," Suzanne answered. "Where were you during the food fight today?"

"I . . . um . . . er . . . I was in the bathroom," Katie stammered. She hated lying to her friend, but she just couldn't tell her what had really happened.

"I can't believe you missed the whole thing," Suzanne continued. "It was amazing. Food was flying all over the place. I don't think I'll ever get the tomato juice off of my sweater. Kevin hit me in the back with a really squishy one!"

"Did it hurt?" Katie asked her.

"Nah," Suzanne said. "It was too mushy to hurt. It just sort of slid down my back. Besides, I got Kevin back—big time! I poured a container of grape juice over his head! His whole face turned purple. He looked like a space alien."

Katie giggled, a little.

"I don't think it's fair that Mrs. Derkman made you clean up with everyone else. You weren't even there." Suzanne continued. "It's such a bummer that you were in the bathroom! Katie, you always miss the good stuff."

"I heard all about it, though," Katie told Suzanne. "The whole school was talking about it when I got back to the cafeteria."

"But I'll bet you don't know what happened *after* the food fight," Suzanne said.

Katie smiled. Suzanne loved knowing things before anybody else did.

"What?" Katie asked her.

"Guess," Suzanne answered.

"Come on, Suzanne. Just tell me," Katie urged.

"Lucille the lunch lady got fired!" Suzanne exclaimed. "Mr. Kane told my mom when she came to pick me up. He said that he couldn't let a lunch lady who acted like an eight-year-old work in the school."

Katie felt guilty all over again.

"The weird thing was, Lucille *was* kinda acting like a kid," Suzanne continued. "I heard she told Malcolm the food belonged in the garbage. She even threw a bunch of it."

"That wasn't any reason to fire her," Katie interrupted her. "The food *is* really gross. We should have healthier stuff to eat."

"I guess," Suzanne agreed.

"And you know what else?" Katie continued. "Lucille didn't even really start the food fight. She was throwing some food out in the garbage and it landed on George by mistake. He started the food fight."

"How do you know that?" Suzanne asked her suddenly. "You weren't even there."

Oops! Katie had forgotten that she was supposed to have been in the girls room during the food fight. "Well, that's what I heard, anyway," she lied. "A bunch of kids said George was the one who yelled out 'food fight!' Maybe Mr. Kane should have fired him instead."

Suzanne laughed. "Mr. Kane can't fire a kid," she told Katie. "Kids have to go to school. It's a law."

"Well, anyway, it wasn't fair of Mr. Kane to fire Lucille," Katie continued.

"Oh who cares?" Suzanne said. "She's just a grouchy lunch lady. Besides, it was her own fault."

"She made a mistake," Katie insisted. "How'd you like it if you got punished every time you made a mistake? Everyone deserves a second chance—even grouches."

"I guess," Suzanne finally agreed. "But what can we do about it? We're just kids."

Katie was quiet for a minute, thinking. Suddenly an idea exploded in her head. "Suzanne, do you think you can bring a bag lunch for school tomorrow?" she asked excitedly.

"Sure, I guess so," Suzanne answered.

"Good. So will I," Katie said. "We have to call everyone we know and ask them to pack their lunches, too. Let's make sure every kid in the whole school brings a bag lunch tomorrow."

"I don't get it," Suzanne admitted. "How is that going to get Lucille her job back?"

"Nobody in our school is going to buy a cafeteria lunch until Lucille is back behind the counter!" Katie explained. "We're on a cafeteria strike!"

As soon as she hung up the phone with Suzanne, Katie called Jeremy and told him about the cafeteria strike. He had to let the boys know not to bring lunch money tomorrow.

"I don't know, Katie. Are you sure the kids will want to help Lucille?" Jeremy asked after Katie explained the plan to him. "She *is* kind of mean."

"Well, we're not so nice to her, either. All we ever do is complain about the food," Katie told him. "And she has a really hard job. It's hot back there in the kitchen. And she's standing up all the time. You wouldn't believe how badly her feet hurt!"

"How do you know that?" Jeremy asked.

Katie gulped. She'd almost let Jeremy know what had happened to her today. She needed to be more careful about what she said. "I . . . um . . . I'm just guessing that's how she feels," she stammered nervously. "Anyway, maybe Lucille would like us better if she knew we'd tried to get her job back for her."

"Maybe," Jeremy agreed. "She probably wouldn't have gotten fired if the food fight hadn't gotten wild. I guess it's kind of partly our fault."

"Exactly," Katie said. "That's why we should do this for her."

"It's worth a try, anyhow," Jeremy agreed. "What do you want me to do?"

"Just call two or three boys in our class and tell them about the strike," Katie instructed him. "Ask them to call a few of their friends. Then those kids can tell more kids, and they can tell more kids. If we keep the chain going all afternoon, by tomorrow everyone will know about the strike."

"I'll try," Jeremy assured Katie. "I hope it works."

"This plan has got to work," Katie answered. "It just has to!"

Chapter 7

The next morning, Katie had a lot of trouble sitting still in class. All she could think about was the cafeteria strike. Katie wasn't sure if all the kids in school had gotten phone calls. She wondered if everyone had agreed to bring their own lunches. If even one kid decided to buy lunch, the plan wouldn't work. They all had to stick together.

Luckily, as soon as she walked into the cafeteria, Katie knew she had nothing to worry about. No one was buying the school lunch. The cafeteria tables were covered with brown bags and lunch boxes the kids had brought from home.

Katie looked toward the counter. There was a new lunch lady standing there. She was short and chubby, with small gray eyes and big, yellow teeth. She looked *really* mean. She also looked really bored. None of the kids were buying lunch. The new lunch lady had nothing to do.

Katie smiled happily as she opened up her lunch bag.

"I thought you said your mom didn't have time to make you lunch in the morning," Suzanne remarked.

"She doesn't," Katie answered. "I made this myself." She took a big bite of her peanut butter and jelly sandwich. "It's pretty good. What do you have?"

Suzanne pulled a small plastic container from her brown bag. Inside the container were six evenly cut pieces of sushi. Suzanne took a pair of chopsticks from the bag and began to eat.

Katie glanced over at the next table where

the boys were sitting. Ever since Suzanne and Jeremy had argued over Speedy, the boys and girls in class 3A sat at separate tables. Katie felt bad about not being able to sit near Jeremy at lunch.

Of all the lunches in the cafeteria, George's was the most amazing. Most of the kids had brought lunch boxes or little brown bags with them to school. But not George. He was carrying a huge brown bag, the kind you got when you brought groceries home from the supermarket. Slowly, he began to empty the bag. First he unpacked a huge hero sandwich. Then he took out a pickle and a container of potato salad. Next he opened his Thermos and poured himself a cup of juice. Finally, he pulled a bag of corn chips out of the bag.

"Wow! That's some lunch!" Kevin exclaimed loud enough for Katie and the other girls to hear. "George, you are such a pig!"

George bit off a huge hunk of his hero and

began to snort. "Look at me, I'm a pig!" he
shouted as he snorted.

"He's not kidding!" Suzanne said. "Only a
pig would talk with his mouth full."

George leaned over toward the girls' table.
He opened his mouth wide so Suzanne and
Katie could see his half-chewed sandwich.
"Hey, Katie Kazoo, check this out. I have
seafood for lunch!" he told her. "Get it? *See*
food?"

Katie giggled. George was definitely gross.
He was also pretty funny.

Katie and George looked at each other nervously.

And then the worst thing happened.

Nobody laughed. NOBODY. The kids just stood there staring at George.

George blushed red. He looked angrily at Katie.

Katie gulped. This was not good.

Quickly, Katie tried to get George to tell another joke. A funnier one this time.

"Don't you wish this was the last day of school, George?" she asked him.

The kids all stared at Katie. Why was she being so nice to George Brennan?

"You know, Katie, there is one school you have to drop out of before you can graduate," George began.

"What school is that?" Katie asked.

"Parachute school," George told her.

Again, nobody laughed. Now Katie was getting really worried.

And then, out of nowhere, Jeremy started

By now Jeremy and Kevin were there, too. Miriam's mother pulled up in her car. Miriam and Mandy leaped out of the backseat. Manny rode up on his bicycle. He locked the ten-speeder to the bike rack and walked over toward the other kids.

Katie looked around. Most of the kids in her class were there. Now she just had to wait for George.

Katie glanced at her watch. School was starting in five minutes. What if George was afraid to show up? The other kids would be sure he was absent because of Speedy. They'd never let him live that down.

Finally, she saw George walking up the hill toward the schoolyard. He was walking very slowly, but he was definitely coming.

"How come you're so late, George?" Katie asked as George joined the group.

"My clock was slow," George replied.

"You'd be slow too, if you'd been running all night."

"Speaking of pigs," George began as he swallowed his food. "What do you get when you mix a pig and an egg?"

"I don't know," Jeremy answered him. "What?"

"*Ham*pty Dumpty!" George exclaimed.

"Good one, George." Jeremy laughed. "I love your jokes."

"I've got a million of 'em!" George assured him. "What rescued Hampty Dumpty when he fell off the wall?"

"What?" Kevin asked.

"A *ham*bulance, of course," George replied. He chuckled really hard at his own joke.

Katie turned toward the food counter. The new lunch lady was still standing there. Her face looked a little sweaty now—probably because there was a lot of steam coming up from the food trays.

Just then, Mr. Kane walked into the cafeteria. The principal looked around the room. He stared at all the lunch boxes and brown paper

bags on the tables. Then he headed toward the
lunch line. Katie watched as Mr. Kane stared
at all the uneaten food.

"What's going on in here?" Mr. Kane asked
the new lunch lady.

"I don't know," she answered him.
"Nobody's buying lunch."

Mr. Kane nodded his head slowly. Then he
turned and faced the kids.

"Okay, kids, what's going on in here? Why
isn't anyone buying lunch?" the principal asked.

" 'Cause we're on strike," a boy from the
kindergarten called out. The grown-up words

sounded funny coming from such a little boy. Everyone started to laugh, even Mr. Kane.

"You are?" Mr. Kane kneeled down next to him. "Why, Joshua?"

" 'Cause the lunch lady went away. We want her back," Josh explained.

Katie smiled as she watched the principal stand up and look around at all the brown bags and lunch boxes in the cafeteria. Now that he understood why the kids weren't buying lunches, Katie was sure the principal was going to tell them that Lucille could have her job back.

Katie sat up straight. She was about to be a hero.

But Katie was wrong. Mr. Kane didn't say a word. He just walked out of the room. Katie slumped down in her seat. This was not going to be as easy as she'd thought.

The students of Cherrydale Elementary School were not quitters. The next day they all brought their own lunches to school again. Once more, the new lunch lady stood all alone behind her trays. She looked even more angry, bored, and sweaty than she had the day before.

Katie took her seat next to Suzanne at the girls' table and opened her lunch bag.

"What do you have today?" Suzanne asked her.

"Peanut butter and jelly," Katie answered.

"Again?" Suzanne said.

Katie shrugged. "It's the only thing I know how to make. What have you got?"

"My mother gave me some leftover pizza with extra cheese," Suzanne said. "I like to eat it cold."

Katie glanced over toward the boys' table. Jeremy had brought a big bag of jelly beans to school. He was busy sharing them with Kevin and Carlos. Katie knew that if she were sitting over there, Jeremy would have let her have some of the purple ones. But the other boys didn't want Katie—or any of the girls—

sitting at their table.

Katie sure wished that Jeremy and Suzanne would stop fighting over the hamster. Their fight was ruining the whole class. Besides, they had to decide something fast. Tomorrow was Friday. Speedy still didn't have a home to go to for the weekend!

Katie also hoped that Mr. Kane would decide to hire Lucille back soon. The cafeteria was really starting to smell because of the strike. Since no one had bought the hot dogs yesterday, the lunch lady had brought them out again. School hot dogs always smelled pretty bad, but *day-old* school hot dogs really stank.

Just then, Mr. Kane walked toward the front of the cafeteria and looked out at the students. "It looks like we have a lot of uneaten food today, just like yesterday," he told them in a loud, stern voice. "I suppose it will be the same way tomorrow, too," he added.

Katie gulped. Mr. Kane sounded a little bit angry about the cafeteria strike. She was also pretty sure he was looking in her direction when he spoke. Did Mr. Kane know that Katie had started the cafeteria strike? Was he going to be angry with her? For the first time, Katie was worried about how the cafeteria strike was going to turn out.

But just then, Mr. Kane's stern frown turned upside down. He smiled at the children. "Well, I have good news for you kids," the principal said. "Lucille and I spoke on the phone today. I told her I thought she deserved a second chance."

Katie smiled. That's what she thought, too.

"You'll all be glad to know that Lucille said she'd come back to work . . . if you all promised to be good at lunch time," Mr. Kane told them.

"Hooray!" The kids in the cafeteria cheered.

"She also made me promise that we would have some better-tasting food and fresher vegetables. Starting tomorrow, we will have a different menu in the cafeteria."

"Hooray!" Once again, the kids began to shout wildly.

Mr. Kane looked sternly at the cheering kids. Everyone got quiet really quickly. "But

your food fight made a big mess of this room. We'll never get these walls completely cleaned up. You kids will have to stay after school for a few days to paint them."

Now the kids looked really sad. Painting the walls sounded like a boring job.

Just then, Katie had an idea. She raised her hand shyly. Mr. Kane looked over at her. "Yes, Katie," he said.

"Do we have to paint the walls this same color? Or can we paint a big picture on the wall instead?" she asked.

Mr. Kane thought about that for a minute. Then he nodded. "That's a wonderful idea, Katie. It would be nice to have a mural that was painted by our students." He smiled at the kids. "This cafeteria strike has proven that you can do great things when you all work together. I can't wait to see what kind of painting you can come up with."

"This is going to be the most beautiful cafeteria ever!" Katie assured the principal.

Chapter 8

The kids in class 3A began planning the mural as soon as Mr. Kane left the cafeteria.

"I think we should have unicorns and stars," Suzanne suggested.

"Oh yeah," Zoe agreed. "That sounds so pretty."

Kevin sat at the boys' table and rolled his eyes. "Would you listen to those girls? Who wants a *pretty* mural? I say we go for cool stuff like skateboards and hot-air balloons."

"Sounds good to me," Jeremy agreed.

"I'm not painting any dumb unicorn," George said.

That did it. Katie got up and stood right

between the two tables.

"Cut it out!" she shouted. "I'm tired of everybody fighting."

"It's her fault," Jeremy said, pointing at Suzanne.

"Are you nuts?" Suzanne shouted. "You started it."

"I don't care who started it," Katie said. "If we keep fighting we won't have any mural at all. We all have to work together."

"Okay, so what's it gonna be, Katie Kazoo? Skateboarders or unicorns?" George asked.

"I don't know," Katie admitted. "Maybe we could come up with something else. Something we're all happy with."

The kids thought about that for a minute.

"Okay," Suzanne agreed.

"You're right, Katie," Jeremy said quietly.

"So we're all friends again?" Katie asked nervously.

"I guess," Jeremy said. He looked across the aisle at Suzanne. "If we keep fighting over

Speedy, he won't have any place to go this weekend. Why don't you take him?"

Katie was surprised. She knew how badly Jeremy had wanted to take Speedy to his house.

Katie was even *more* surprised by Suzanne's answer.

"No, he's better off with you," Suzanne said. "Heather's stuff is pretty much all over my whole house. Everywhere you look there's a stroller or a changing table or a crib. I don't think there'd be any room for a hamster playground."

"But you know I have that big game on Saturday. I'm going to be busy with that," Jeremy told her.

Katie was worried all over again. Now it didn't sound like *either* of her friends wanted to take Speedy home. She had to do something fast!

"I have an idea," Katie said quickly. "Jeremy, you keep Speedy at your place.

Suzanne can come over on Saturday morning to give him his food and water while you're at the game."

"That's a good idea," Suzanne agreed. "Hey, and maybe on Sunday we could build him a hamster playground . . . together."

"Cool!" Jeremy exclaimed. "You know, my dad has a huge shoe box. It could be a cave."

"I'll bring over some paper towel rolls for Speedy to climb through," Suzanne said.

Katie sat quietly as she listened to Jeremy

 and Suzanne's plans for the hamster playground. She was really happy that her two best friends were getting along so well. She was also kind of sad. They were leaving her out of everything!

Jeremy guessed how Katie was feeling.

"Can you come over and help us build the playground?" he asked her.

Now Katie smiled brightly. "You bet!" she exclaimed.

Lunchtime was a whole lot more fun the next day. Katie stood on the lunch line right between her two best friends. It was nice not to have to choose between them any more.

When she reached the front of the line, Katie smiled brightly at Lucille. "I'll have a veggie wimpy and a cow juice," she told the lunch Lady. "And for dessert I'd like an Eve with a lid."

Lucille looked at Katie with surprise. She had no idea where the third grader had learned the secret lunchroom language, but she gave Katie a veggie burger, a container of milk, and a slice of apple pie anyway.

"Thanks," Katie told her. "It's good to have you back."

Lucille didn't say anything, but Katie thought she saw her smile a little.

As Katie followed Jeremy to a table near the back of the cafeteria, she felt a slight breeze blowing on the back of her neck. Katie looked around nervously. Was she about to change into someone else . . . right here in front of the whole school?

As Katie looked around, she noticed that the door to the playground was wide open. This was no magic wind. It was just a normal, everyday, outside kind of wind. Katie wasn't changing into anyone. She was staying Katie Kazoo.

At least for now.

Yummy Lunch Recipies!

Do you find the same old peanut-butter-and-jelly sandwiches in your lunch box every day? Are you sick of hard-boiled eggs and tuna salad? Well, here's the cure to the boring food blues. These easy-to-make lunch recipes are favorites of the kids in room 3A. Try them all. They're guaranteed to tickle your taste buds!

And after you've filled the inside of your lunch bag with these tasty treats, don't forget about the outside of the bag. Decorate your paper bag with stickers or funny pictures, just to make lunch time more special!

Cracker Stacker

You will need: round crackers, peanut butter, grape jelly.

Here's what you do: Start with a plain cracker. Spread peanut butter on the cracker. Put a second cracker on top of the first.

Spread jelly on the second cracker. Put a third cracker on top of the second cracker. Spread peanut butter on that one. Then top that cracker with a fourth cracker. Spread jelly on the top cracker. Keep going until you have a stack of crackers. Wrap your cracker stack in waxed paper before putting it in your lunch box.

Banana Dogs

You will need: one banana, a hot dog roll, peanut butter.

Here's what you do: Place the banana in the hot dog roll. Smear the banana with peanut butter just the way you would smear mustard on a hot dog. Wrap up your banana dog in waxed paper and pack it in your lunch bag.

Inside-Out Sandwiches

You will need: one slice of bologna (use soy bologna slices if you're a vegetarian like Katie), one slice of American cheese, cream cheese, peanut butter, two bread sticks.

Here's what you do: Lay out the slices of bologna and cheese. Spread cream cheese on one side of the balogna. Spread peanut butter on one side of the American cheese slice. Take one bread stick and wrap the meat around it. Make sure the cream cheese side is touching the bread stick. Wrap the American cheese slice around the second bread stick. Make sure the peanut butter side is touching the bread stick. Now you have two inside-out sandwiches. (The bread [stick]) is in the middle. Get it?) Place the sandwiches in a sealed sandwich bag and pack them in your lunch bag.

Shape-up Sandwiches

You will need: cream cheese, two slices of white or whole-wheat bread, raisins, grape jelly, cookie cutters.

Here's what you do: Spread cream cheese on one slice of bread. Sprinkle raisins on top of the cream cheese. Spread grape jelly on the other slice of bread. Place that slice on top of the raisins and cream cheese with the jelly-side-down. Use the cookie cutters to cut your sandwich into different shapes. Place your shaped sandwiches into plastic bags to keep them fresh.

A Gobble Gobble Good Sandwich

You will need: mayonnaise, three slices of white or whole wheat bread, two slices of turkey (or soy turkey), cranberry sauce, leftover stuffing.

Here's what you do: Spread a thin layer of mayonnaise on one slice of bread. Top the mayonnaise with turkey slices. Add the next slice of bread. Spread cranberry sauce on top of the bread. Place the stuffing on top of the cranberry sauce. Top with the last piece of bread. Store the sandwich in a plastic bag.